Twisted Journeys™ #3

Terror in Ghost Mansion

Paul D. Storrie

ILLUSTRATED BY Sandy Carruthers

GRAPHIC UNIVERSE · MINNEAPOLIS

Story by Paul D. Storrie

Pencils and inks by Sandy Carruthers

Coloring by Hi-Fi Design

Lettering by Marshall Dillon and Terri Delgado

Graphic Universe
A division of Lerner Publishing Group, Inc.
241 First Avenue North
Minneapolis, MN 55401 U.S.A.

Website address: www.lernerbooks.com

Library of Congress Cataloging-in-Publication Data

Storrie, Paul D.
      Terror in Ghost Mansion / by Paul D. Storrie ; illustrations by Sandy Carruthers.
         p.   cm. — (Twisted journeys)
      ISBN 978-0-8225-6776-9 (lib. bdg. : alk. paper)
      1. Graphic novels. I. Carruthers, Sandy. II. Title.
   PN6727.S746T47 2007
   741.5'973—dc22   2006101597

Manufactured in the United States of America
1 2 3 4 5 6 – DP – 12 11 10 09 08 07

ARE YOU READY FOR YOUR

THE PLACE: AN OLD, SPOOKY HOUSE
THAT JUST MIGHT BE HAUNTED.
THE TIME: A VERY DARK
HALLOWEEN NIGHT.
THE HERO: *YOU!*

EACH PAGE TELLS WHAT HAPPENS TO *YOU*
AS YOU EXPLORE GHOST MANSION, DISGUISED IN
YOUR MUMMY COSTUME. *YOUR* WORDS AND
THOUGHTS ARE SHOWN IN THE *YELLOW BALLOONS.*
JUST FOLLOW THE NOTE AT THE BOTTOM OF EACH
PAGE UNTIL YOU REACH A *Twisted Journeys™* PAGE.
THEN MAKE THE CHOICE *YOU* LIKE BEST.

BUT BE CAREFUL...THE WRONG CHOICE COULD *HAUNT*
YOU FOR THE REST OF YOUR LIFE!

"I should just take you home," Barry growls from the driver's seat. He's mad that his parents are making him haul his younger brother Tim, you, and your friend Sue to a big Halloween party. Plus, it's just started raining.

"Look out!" Tim screams.

"Whoa!" yelps Barry, jerking the steering wheel to the right. Through the car window, you see a boy standing in the road, lit by the headlights.

The car skids on the wet pavement. It slides into a ditch.

You all scramble out. Everyone seems okay.

"Where's the kid?" asks Tim.

"We didn't hit him," says Barry.

"Probably got scared and ran home," you say.

Barry tries to use his cell phone to call a tow truck. It isn't working.

Up the hill, you see a light flickering in the window of a big house. Pointing, you say, "Maybe they can help us up there."

THE RAIN SOAKS YOU AS YOU GO UP THE HILL. THEN THE LIGHTNING STARTS.

KRAKA-BOOM!

GOOD EVENING. WHAT...INTERESTING CLOTHES.

WE SLID INTO A DITCH!

CAN WE USE YOUR PHONE?

WE WERE ON OUR WAY TO A HALLOWEEN PARTY.

WELCOME TO THE HALE HOUSE. PLEASE, COME IN.

I'M AFRAID WE HAVE NO WORKING PHONE AT PRESENT. NOR ELECTRICITY, AS YOU CAN SEE.

WE APPRECIATE YOU LETTING US IN OUT OF THE RAIN, MR. HALE.

MY NAME IS HILLER. DR. HALE IS MY EMPLOYER.

HE TOLD ME I SHOULD ASK YOU TO STAY THE NIGHT. WE HAVE PLENTY OF ROOMS.

UNLESS YOU WOULD PREFER TO STAY IN YOUR VEHICLE?

GO ON TO THE NEXT PAGE.

5

YOU QUICKLY TELL HIM THAT YOU'D RATHER NOT. HE TAKES YOU UP A CREAKING SET OF STAIRS.

THERE IS ONE FOR EACH OF YOU, OF COURSE. **DR. HALE** WOULD **NOT** BE PLEASED IF YOU TRIED TO **SHARE** A ROOM.

PLEASE EXCUSE THE DUST. WE DON'T OFTEN HAVE GUESTS.

WHERE'S DR. HALE?

THE DOCTOR AND HIS FAMILY WILL VISIT YOU A BIT LATER. UNTIL THEN, PLEASE STAY IN YOUR ROOMS.

THIS PLACE IS CREEPY. I DON'T WANT TO STAY ALONE.

DON'T BE A BABY. IT'S JUST AN OLD HOUSE!

HUH. IT ALMOST SOUNDED LIKE HE **WANTED** US TO STAY IN THE CAR.

GO ON TO THE NEXT PAGE.

Tim really wants everyone to stay together.
But would that make Dr. Hale angry?
What if he sends you back out in the storm?

WILL YOU . . .

. . . say you should stick together?
TURN TO PAGE 36.

. . . say you should each
go to your own room?
TURN TO PAGE 54.

You creep down the stairs as quietly as you can. You're grateful that they're stone. No creaking boards.

At the bottom of the steps, you find another round room. This one has several big leather chairs with little round tables next to them.

A heavy wooden door with iron bands across it seems to be the only exit.

Very carefully, you lift the latch on the door. Pulling it open just a little, you peer through the crack.

It opens into a game room. In the center is an old-fashioned billiards table, with nets in the corner for pockets. The balls are all inside a triangle-shaped rack sitting in the middle of the table.

Past the table, there's a set of doors that slide into the wall on either side. Pocket doors, you think they're called.

There's no sign of the . . . the ghosts.

You don't hear anyone. Maybe you're safe here. It doesn't look like anyone has been in the tower for a long time. Then again, it's not like ghosts would leave footprints.

WILL YOU . . .

. . . try to sneak out through the game room?

TURN TO PAGE 80.

. . . try hiding out in the tower?

TURN TO PAGE 105.

"Tim's right!" you scream. Rushing over to the curtains, you grab the glass chimney off the candle. Then you put the flame right up next to the dusty, dry cloth.

"Hold it right there!" you yell at the ghosts. They're just a step or two away from Sue. "Let us out of here or I'll light these curtains and your house will burn down!"

Dr. Hale looks almost impressed and says, "I see only one flaw in your plan."

"Oh, yeah?" sneers Tim. "What's that?"

"I can light small fires," the doctor replies. "And I can put them out."

He snaps his spectral fingers. Suddenly, your candle and all the lamps go out. The whole house is plunged into darkness.

You hear Sue gasp.

Tim calls out for his brother.

Then, right next to you, a voice says, "Boo!"

You stumble away from the noise. In the dark, you don't get far.

THE END

As you look across
your room, you see the
lightning flashing
beyond the window. It
occurs to you that if you
climb out and stretch
down, holding onto the windowsill, it will only be a few
feet to the ground! The ledge
behind the house isn't very wide,
but it should be wide enough.

You grab the chair and, straining
with the effort, toss it through the glass.

The window explodes into a million shimmering shards.

You rush over, brushing away the last of the glass with
your bandaged hands.

Your heart pounds as you look down. Your eyes can't help
looking past the ledge below, down the deep, dark chasm
beyond.

Maybe you should try to use the bedspread to let yourself
down?

GO ON TO THE NEXT PAGE.

You're not sure you have the time to grab
the bedspread and tie it to something.
Still, it's a long way to the ground.

WILL YOU . . .

. . . grab the bedspread to use as a rope?
TURN TO PAGE 25.

. . . forget about the bedspread
and climb down now?
TURN TO PAGE 48.

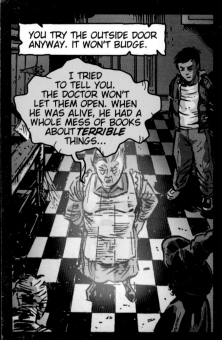

YOU TRY THE OUTSIDE DOOR ANYWAY. IT WON'T BUDGE.

I TRIED TO TELL YOU. THE DOCTOR WON'T LET THEM OPEN. WHEN HE WAS ALIVE, HE HAD A WHOLE MESS OF BOOKS ABOUT *TERRIBLE* THINGS...

IRIS!

HOW COULD YOU?

HOW DARE YOU TALK ABOUT MY HUSBAND'S BUSINESS?!

AAAIIIIIEEEE!

SHE TRIED TO HELP YOU, BUT YOU KNOW THERE'S NOTHING YOU CAN DO FOR HER. YOU RUN.

GO ON TO THE NEXT PAGE.

You look around the room. It's a parlor with fancy chairs and flimsy tables. The windows are dark. A flash of lightning just barely shows beyond the heavy wooden shutters.

There's an archway that opens into the front hall! You run that way.

"I thought there was another of you."

The boy from down in the road is standing in the front hall. He crosses his arms and scowls.

"I didn't get you to come here to play with my mother!" he grumbles.

You skid to a stop, the floor creaking beneath your feet. You look for another way out. You look at the staircase. Then you see a tall, thin man standing on the balcony. "Now, now, Chester," he says. "You know your mother isn't well. Besides, she's busy in the kitchen now."

The ghost boy gives you a nasty smile. "That means you're all mine!"

THE END

The door pivots open with a gentle push, but it scrapes and creaks as it opens. You cringe, hoping no one heard. You push it closed, cringing again at the noise.

The flickering light of your candle lights up a round room with bookcases from the ceiling to the floor. The shelves are crammed with books of all shapes and sizes. In the center of the room, there's a big wooden table with more books lying open on it. The whole place smells musty. There's dust on everything.

There are two stone staircases. The one on the right leads up. The one on the left leads down.

You remember that there was a tower on one end of the house. This must be it.

GO ON TO THE NEXT PAGE.

There are no exits from the tower, so going up or down these stairs won't get you any closer to escaping. But it might be a good way to hide.

WILL YOU . . .

. . . go down the tower stairs?
TURN TO PAGE 8.

. . . go up the tower stairs?
TURN TO PAGE 69.

. . . go back into the secret passage?
TURN TO PAGE 109.

"You must be crazy if you think I'd trust a ghost!" you yell. Then you dart through the nearest doorway, away from her.

"Come back," she hisses. "They'll get you for sure!"

You ignore her and look around the room you've just run into. It's a parlor, with dainty furniture and doilies all over everything. There's an archway to your left leading to the front hallway.

Dashing through the archway, you skid to a stop in front of the doors. The floor creaks under your feet. Grabbing the doorknob of the nearest one, you twist it and tug with all your might. It won't budge.

"There you are!" says a voice behind you.

You turn to see the pale little boy drifting down the stairs. "My father has shut the house until morning. You can't leave."

GO ON TO THE NEXT PAGE.

YOUR *FRIENDS* WERE A LOT OF FUN. *YOU* JUST KEEP RUNNING AWAY.

REMEMBERING WHAT HAPPENED TO YOUR FRIENDS, YOU DECIDE TO KEEP RUNNING! THE FLOOR CREAKS AND GROANS UNDER YOUR FEET.

IF ONLY YOU KNEW A SAFE PLACE TO RUN *TO*! MAYBE THE KITCHEN. MAYBE IRIS WILL STILL HELP!

BUT MAYBE YOU SHOULD JUST HIDE AND TRY TO SNEAK BACK THE WAY YOU CAME AFTER THE GHOST BOY GOES BY.

GO ON TO THE NEXT PAGE.

You might have made a mistake not trusting Iris. Is it too late? Maybe she can't help you now that the ghost boy is right behind you.

WILL YOU . . .

. . . head for the kitchen and hope Iris can still help?

TURN TO PAGE 45.

. . . try to find a place to hide?

TURN TO PAGE 65.

Yanking the glass cover off the candle, you set the couch on fire! Old and dry, it catches quickly.

"Put it out!" Mrs. Hale shrieks at her husband.

"It's too much!" he screams back. "I can only control small flames!"

The front door flies open. "Go!" shouts the ghost. "Push the couch out of here and you're free! But try to leave first and the door will shut. You'll burn with the house!"

Grabbing the far end of the couch, you all heave it towards to front hall. Foot by foot, it scrapes along the floor.

A cold breeze fans the fire as you shove the couch out the door and off the porch. You're safe . . .

. . . until the kid you almost ran over floats out of the house!

"Father lied," he says. "Now we can play."

"Run!" you shout.

You don't stop until you're far, far away from the terrors of Ghost Mansion.

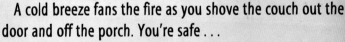

THE END

GO ON TO THE NEXT PAGE.

Barry runs to the front door. The floor in the front hallway creaks and moans under his feet.

He pulls with all his strength, but the door won't open. "It's locked too!" he screams.

"What do we do?!" yells Tim.

Just then, Mrs. Hale comes drifting through the door leading from the dining room. She looks just as pale and ragged as the doctor.

"Poor frightened bunnies," she groans. "Running and hopping and scurrying away. Not for long. Not for long."

"They're all ghosts!" you shout.

"Hurry!" cries Tim. "Upstairs!"

"The doctor said that the little guy is up there," you remind him. "That's probably who we heard in the hall!"

Beyond Barry is an archway leading into another room. "Through there!" you say.

Both Mrs. Hale and her husband drift nearer, closing in.

GO ON TO THE NEXT PAGE.

You don't know which way to go,
but you'd better decide fast!

WILL YOU . . .

. . . run into the next room?
TURN TO PAGE 42.

. . . take your chances upstairs?
TURN TO PAGE 98.

You run back to the bed. As you grab the bedspread, a shiver runs down your spine.

The ghost of Dr. Hale is oozing through the wall.

"What a MESS," he grumbles. "Now Hiller will have to clean this up."

Dropping the bedspread, you run to the window.

You climb out as fast as you can. As you lower yourself from the windowsill, Dr. Hale smiles down at you.

"I have good news and bad news for you," he says. "The good news is that I cannot leave this house, the place where I died. I can't even reach out the window."

You let out a sigh of relief.

"The bad news is that when I was alive, I learned a few tricks with fire."

Suddenly, the bandages on your hands burst into flames!

The pain makes you let go of the windowsill. You tumble down, falling into the dark chasm behind Ghost Mansion.

THE END

YOU ASK HER TO TELL YOU MORE ABOUT WHAT'S GOING ON IN THIS PLACE.

THERE ISN'T MUCH TIME. I'LL TRY TO KEEP IT SHORT...

tHE DOCTOR FANCIED HIMSELF SOMETHING OF A SORCERER, YOU SEE. COLLECTED ALL SORTS OF BOOKS THAT ONE SHOULDN'T.

MAYBE THAT'S WHY CHESTER TURNED OUT TO BE SUCH A BAD ONE. USED TO JUMP OUT IN FRONT OF PEOPLE DOWN ON THE ROAD TO MAKE THEM WRECK THEIR AUTOMOBILES!

ONE DAY, A DRIVER COULDN'T STOP. RAN THE BOY DOWN. MRS. HALE WENT BATTY. THE DOCTOR TRIED TO HELP HER OUT WITH HOCUS POCUS FROM THOSE BOOKS...

26

GO ON TO THE NEXT PAGE.

"Iris!" a shriek interrupts her story.

You turn to see Mrs. Hale standing in the room, her arms thrown up in outrage. You didn't even hear her come in.

"How dare you share my husband's private business!" she moans. "How could you betray us like this?"

Clutching her hands to her chest, Mrs. Hale starts to wail.

"I'm so sorry," Iris sobs to you as she fades away.

The wailing gets louder. It's like nails on a chalkboard, but ten times worse. You clamp your hands on your ears, but it doesn't help.

Your head pounds with the thumping of your heart.

The pounding stops, but the screaming doesn't.

THE END

"What do I do?" you ask.

"The sunroom is on the other side of the dining room there. Lots of windows and no shutters at all. Smash a few and get on out of here!"

You thank her and dash through the door.

The dining room is huge, with a long table set with plates, silverware, platters, and glasses. There's no food. No one here has eaten in a long time.

Back in the kitchen, you hear a woman shriek, "Iris! Where did the little scamp go?"

Then you're out the other door and into a room with a whole wall of tall windows.

The chairs here are wicker. They look frail from all the years they've been sitting unused. Small wooden tables sit near a few of the chairs.

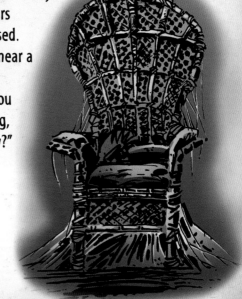

From the next room, you hear a child's voice calling, "Mother! Where's my toy?"

GO ON TO THE NEXT PAGE.

The creepy kid is really close! Maybe you should just take a running jump and smash right through the glass. But can you do that without getting cut?

WILL YOU . . .

. . . go ahead and jump?
TURN TO PAGE 62.

. . . take the time to smash the window?
TURN TO PAGE 102.

"Tim's right!" you say, grabbing the candle from the table. You slip inside the fireplace. Tim is right behind you. After a couple seconds, Barry and Sue follow.

Inside, there's a lever. When you pull it, the back of the fireplace slides forward, shutting you in.

"This is crazy!" says Sue. "Now what are we supposed to do?"

"Just follow the passage," says Barry. "There's got to be another way out."

"I just want to find the door that gets me out of this creepy place!" says Tim.

You lead the way down the pas-  sage. There are other openings like the one you came through, each with its own lever. You're pretty sure they just lead into the rooms your friends were sup- posed to stay in.

You pass them by. The four of you walk quietly down the passageway by the flickering light of your candle.

HANG ON, WHAT'S THIS?

TOO WEIRD.

BARRY MOVES OUT OF THE WAY SO YOU CAN LOOK TOO.

WHERE HAS SWEET LITTLE *CHESTER* GONE, FREDERICK? I GET SO SAD WHEN HE GOES AWAY...

NEVER FEAR, BEVERLY. HE'S JUST GONE UP TO PLAY WITH OUR GUESTS. HE'LL BE DOWN WHEN HE'S DONE WITH THEM.

GO ON TO THE NEXT PAGE.

After Tim and Sue have had a chance to look too, Barry closes the panel.

"I wonder if Chester was the kid down in the road?" whispers Barry.

"How come they're dressed like that?" hisses Tim.

"Hello," Sue says quietly. "It's Halloween. Maybe they just got back from a costume party? We should just go back to our rooms and stop acting like scared little kids."

"I don't know," you say. "That lady seems kind of loopy. Let's just follow this passage and see where it goes."

You continue down the dark, cramped corridor for what seems like forever.

Eventually, you come to a set of narrow stairs, leading down. There's also a door off to one side.

"What now?" you ask.

GO ON TO THE NEXT PAGE.

Barry wants to take the stairs. Tim is getting twitchy about being stuck in such a cramped space. "Let's use the door!" he says.

WILL YOU . . .

. . . go down the steps?
TURN TO PAGE 93.

. . . get out of the passage right away?
TURN TO PAGE 106.

GO ON TO THE NEXT PAGE.

As you run across the dining room, Mrs. Hale rises from the chair at the other end of the table.

"What are you doing?!" she shouts.

Suddenly she changes, like her husband did.

"NO RUNNING IN THE HOUSE!" she howls. Then she begins to moan and wail. The sound is awful! Tim stops, but Barry runs into him. They both fall.

On the floor, Tim rolls into a ball, covering his ears. Barry grabs hold of his brother and tries to drag him away.

Sue spins around and slams into you. You stumble back. Suddenly, you feel an icy cold fill your chest.

You fall to the ground. As your sight goes dark, you see Dr. Hale over you. Behind him, high on the wall, is a life-size portrait of the doctor himself. It's in just the right place for his eyes to be the ones you looked through from the secret passage.

It seems funny, but you're too cold to laugh.

THE END

"Tim's right," you say. "Something strange is going on. Let's stay together."

"Fine," says Barry. "Everybody in." When you're all inside, he closes the door.

Still nervous, Tim starts poking around the room, looking at the books on the bookshelf and checking the dresser drawers. They're empty.

"He wasn't kidding about the dust," Tim says. "Yuck."

Sue points at the fireplace. "Talk about 'yuck'!" she says.

In the middle of the fireplace mantle, a short stone statue of a gargoyle grins down. Tim tries to haul it down for a closer look. It tilts forward, as if on a hinge, and a hollow click surprises you.

Inside the fireplace, you hear a slight scraping sound. The back slides slowly away, revealing a narrow passageway off to one side.

"That's weird," you say. Just then, you hear quiet giggling out in the hall.

GO ON TO THE NEXT PAGE.

Tim is really scared. Even Sue looks a little nervous.

WILL YOU . . .

. . . try to hide in the secret passage?
TURN TO PAGE 30.

. . . see who is in the hall?
TURN TO PAGE 82.

You push the door closed behind you. "Let's just stay here," you tell the others. "If anyone comes, we'll just say we got lost."

Sue snorts but doesn't say anything.

You all sit down and try to get comfortable.

Suddenly you shiver, like someone's dropped ice down your back.

"W-what was that?" Tim asks.

The candle flickers.

"So THERE you are!" says a high-pitched voice behind you.

You all spin around. The boy from the road is standing there, a wicked grin on his lips. You didn't hear him come in.

"Father doesn't like it when people come here," he says.

As he comes towards you, you notice you can almost see THROUGH him.

"H-he's a g-g-gho . . ." you stammer as the boy's pale hands reach INTO your chest. It feels like he's jabbed an icicle through your heart.

The last thing you hear is your friends screaming your name.

THE END

TWISTED JOURNEYS™

You know that you need to get to the ground floor eventually, but that's probably what the ghosts are expecting you to do. Maybe you should just go out the door?

WILL YOU . . .

. . . go through the door?
TURN TO PAGE 16.

. . . go down the stairs?
TURN TO PAGE 47.

"I think he's just trying to scare us," you whisper to the others. "Maybe if we're not afraid, we'll be okay."

Sue stops screaming. She looks embarrassed. "Really?" she asks softly.

Barry frowns. "I don't know."

Tim stares at you for a second. Then he laughs. "Cool."

Taking a deep breath, you walk over to the little ghost.

"L-look," you say, "we're not scared of you. Why don't you go find someone else to spook?"

He looks up at you with sad eyes. "Really? Are you sure?"

You cross your arms and try to look confident. "Absolutely."

"Oh well," he says. Then he reaches out his small, pale hand and sticks it right into your forehead! Gasping, you try to pull away. It's like icicles in your brain!

The others start to scream. You can barely hear the ghost boy say, "Maybe they'll be more fun."

THE END

"I don't know what happens when a ghost touches you—and I don't want to find out!" you say, pulling Sue along with you into the next room.

It's big, with a couple of couches and lots of chairs. There's even a piano.

"We have to get out of here!" shouts Barry. He picks up the piano bench and throws it at the window.

Glass shatters as the bench hits the window. There's a loud *crack* as the bench bounces off the closed shutters beyond the broken glass. The bench tumbles to the floor in pieces.

Suddenly, a shiver runs along your spine. The butler fades into view, a sad look on his face.

"I'd better get something to clean that up," he says. Then he drifts off towards the back of the house. "Perhaps you should have stayed in your automobile," the butler sighs.

GO ON TO THE NEXT PAGE.

TWISTED JOURNEYS™

Maybe Tim's plan is the best one. But you suddenly wonder how the ghosts lit all these candles in the first place.

WILL YOU . . .

. . . follow Tim's suggestion and threaten to start a fire with your candle?

TURN TO PAGE 10.

. . . forget the threats and use the candle to start a fire as quickly as you can?

TURN TO PAGE 21.

. . . let Sue prove that ghosts can't hurt people?

TURN TO PAGE 46.

. . . help Barry throw the chair at the shutters?

TURN TO PAGE 71.

You run toward the kitchen as fast as you can. Maybe Iris can help you hide or something.

Behind you, you hear Chester whining. "I'm getting bored!"

You just run faster.

You rush through the kitchen door, calling out, "I'm sorry! I should have trusted you! Help me!"

Then you see who's waiting for you.

It's the ghostly man and woman from the upstairs hall. Dr. and Mrs. Hale. They look angry.

"We had a little talk with Iris," says Dr. Hale. "She should know better than to interfere with Chester's fun."

Mrs. Hale spreads her arms wide as she lunges towards you. "Run along and play!" she shrieks.

You stumble back through the door you just came in. Chester is right there. You run right through him.

Icy cold washes over your whole body. Your legs stop working. You tumble to the floor.

Chester peers down at you, grinning madly. "That was funny," he says.

THE END

"Relax, guys," you say. "Sue's probably right. They just pass right through stuff!"

Sue wags her finger at the ghosts. "You should be ashamed, frightening us like this."

"That's what ghosts do," Dr. Hale replies.

"Well, it's not going to work anymore!" Sue tells him, jabbing her finger at him to make the point.

The ghost reaches out, grabbing Sue's wrist. The ghostly fingers seem to sink into her arm.

She was right!

Then Sue starts to shiver. Her arm begins to turn bluish gray. "Wha—?" she gasps. She tries to pull away, but the ghost just moves with her.

The other ghosts swoop towards you, Barry, and Tim, laughing.

"It seems we're not so harmless after all," the doctor chuckles.

THE END

You make your way cautiously down the stairs. At the bottom, there's a narrow door.

Slowly, you push it open. The hinges don't squeal. Much.

You step through and find yourself in a kitchen. Slowly, carefully, you swing the panel shut.

There's a woman standing behind it!

You gulp.

She raises a finger to her lips. You realize she's shorter and heavier than the ghost lady from upstairs. She's wearing a white apron over her plain dress.

"I think they're still upstairs," she whispers.

You realize you can almost see through her. "You're one of them!"

"Don't be afraid of old Iris," she says quietly. "The doctor done something unpleasant to keep me and Mr. Hiller around. Doesn't mean we have to like it! You can trust us."

"I can show you how to get out," she says, "but I'd appreciate if you'd help us out first."

TURN TO PAGE 49.

TURN TO PAGE 61.

You wonder if this is some kind of trick. Iris seems nice, but how can you know for sure?

WILL YOU . . .

. . . just try to get away?
TURN TO PAGE 18.

. . . trust her, but ask her to help you leave right away?
TURN TO PAGE 74.

. . . try to help her before you escape?
TURN TO PAGE 111.

"I'm sorry," you say, "but I'm worried that they'll find me before I do what you ask."

Iris nods, sadly.

"Maybe I can come back," you tell her. "But right now I have to get away. My friends . . . our parents . . . "

"I understand, child," she says. "Come along. I'll get you out of here."

She gestures for you to follow her. Her head hangs low as she drifts slowly towards the door to the dining room. Then she pauses, turning back to you.

"It's just that we've been here for so long," she says. "And there have been others, like you and your friends. But if Hiller and I try to help, and the Hales find out . . . " She shudders. "They do awful things to us."

"Iris!" a woman's voice calls out from the kitchen. "Where are you?"

"Mrs. Hale!" gasps Iris. "We have to hurry!"

GO ON TO THE NEXT PAGE.

You lie on the floor, shivering, unable to stand or crawl. The ghost boy drifts into the room, frowning.

"Mother and father are going to be very cross with you, Iris, "he says.

Wailing in despair, Iris drifts out of sight.

Chester sits down, cross-legged, in midair.

"She went through you very quickly," he says, "and she didn't want to hurt you. I bet you'll be able to move before very long."

He puts one elbow on his knee and then rests his chin in his hand. "Maybe I'll just wait so I can chase you some more."

For a few long moments, he sits quietly, watching you.

"This is boring," he sighs. "I guess I don't want to wait after all."

Reaching down, he plunges his pale hand inside your chest. You can almost feel ghostly fingers clutching at your heart . . .

THE END

This is starting to sound more complicated than you expected. What if the other ghosts catch you before you can do what Iris asks?

WILL YOU . . .

. . . ask her for more information?
TURN TO PAGE 26.

. . . tell her you think it's too risky?
TURN TO PAGE 50.

. . . just do what she asks?
TURN TO PAGE 85.

"Come on, Tim," you say. "It's only a few hours. What could happen?"

Tim opens his mouth to reply, but Barry interrupts.

"Worried about the bogeyman, Tim?" He laughs.

"I don't know about the rest of you, but I'm more worried about what my parents are going to say tomorrow than staying in a spooky house overnight," says Sue.

"Maybe Barry's cell phone will work when the storm passes," you say.

One by one, your friends leave. Soon you're alone in a room lit only by candlelight and the occasional flash of lightning. You wish you could take off your costume, but you've got nothing else to wear. Funny that the butler didn't at least give you some towels to dry off.

Despite what you told Tim, you're too nervous to sleep. You walk over to the window and look out into the dark.

GO ON TO THE NEXT PAGE.

TWISTED JOURNEYS™

You head for the door, then pause. Maybe you should take something with you. Something you could use as a weapon. Do you have time?

WILL YOU . . .

. . . find something
to defend yourself?
TURN TO PAGE 66.

. . . go right into the hall?
TURN TO PAGE 104.

You shove frantically against the door. It pivots open, creaking and scraping loudly. The sound echoes down the passage and in the room you stumble into. You run into a heavy table, knocking several books to the floor.

Dim light is filtering in from somewhere. You can just make out a round room, with bookcases that go from the floor to the ceiling. They're crammed with strange-looking books of every size and shape. It smells musty, and the thick dust makes you think no one has been here in a long time.

You can just make out a stone staircase leading upward and another leading down.

Suddenly, a thin man in a dark suit oozes through the door!

He's between you and the staircase leading up. You plunge down the other stairs.

Behind you, you hear him shout, "Here, now! I don't allow anyone in my private library!"

GO ON TO THE NEXT PAGE.

HE DOESN'T SEEM TO BE ABLE TO MOVE ANY FASTER THAN YOU CAN RUN. IF YOU CAN JUST REACH THE DOOR...

HAHAHAHAHA HAHAHAHAHA

YOUR BANDAGED HANDS FUMBLE AWKWARDLY WITH THE LATCH. YOU CAN'T HELP THINKING YOU MIGHT DIE BECAUSE OF A HALLOWEEN COSTUME!

IT'S NO USE. THERE'S NOWHERE FOR YOU TO RUN!

FINALLY, THE DOOR OPENS!

With the ghostly man right behind you, you stagger into the game room. You don't even try to go around the billiard table. You just dive underneath.

Scrambling to the door, you glance back to see the man floating THROUGH the table!

Desperately, you throw open the doors, hoping you can stay ahead of him.

You stop.

A thin, ghostly woman in a frilly, white dress is standing on the other side of the door, looking sad. She opens her mouth and begins to wail.

The noise is awful and terrifying. You clap your hands over your ears, but it doesn't help.

Falling to the ground, the only thing you can hear besides the scream is the pounding of your heart. You just wish it would stop.

The screaming doesn't, but your heart does.

THE END

"What happened to my friend?" you say, reaching down to grab the creepy little guy by his jacket. "Did you do something to him?"

Your can't believe your eyes when your hand passes right through him. It feels like you just dunked it in ice water.

"W-what ARE you?" you manage to sputter.

"What do you THINK?" he replies. Then he starts to laugh.

Reaching out a small, pale hand, he pushes it against your stomach. You feel it sink beneath your skin!

A wave of cold washes over you.

You try to call out, to tell Barry and Sue to run. You can't make a sound.

THE END

You're not sure if you can make your way along the ledge without falling. Maybe you should take a minute to calm down. After all, you're outside. Ghosts can't leave the place where they died, can they?

WILL YOU . . .

. . . take a moment to calm down and catch your breath?
TURN TO PAGE 70.

. . . take your chances going now?
TURN TO PAGE 88.

YOU DECIDE THERE'S NO TIME TO WASTE.

KLILLIISSSH!!

TOO LATE, YOU REMEMBER THE CLIFF BEHIND THE HOUSE. THE NARROW LEDGE...

FUNNY. ALL THAT GLASS AND YOU DIDN'T EVEN GET A SCRATCH.

THE END

You struggle to lift the chair. You stagger a few steps and toss it through the glass.

The window explodes into a million shimmering shards.

Then you run back and slip into the passage, hoping they'll think you climbed out the window!

There's just enough light leaking in from the room for you to make out a lever on the wall. You pull it. The fireplace starts to scrape closed.

Then you hear a man's voice say, "What a MESS! Where . . . ah, the secret passage! Clever, child! But not quick enough!"

In a blind panic, you stumble along the dark passageway, occasionally bumping into walls. An eerie wailing echoes behind you.

After what seems like forever, you see a dim light shining under the crack of a door. It's just enough to reveal that there's a staircase leading down, too.

GO ON TO THE NEXT PAGE.

TWISTED JOURNEYS™

What you should do? To get out of the house, you'll have to go downstairs eventually. But in the dark, cramped stairway, you might not see something coming.

WILL YOU . . .

. . . use the door and get out of the passage now?
TURN TO PAGE 57.

. . . go down the stairs?
TURN TO PAGE 91.

The only place you see to hide is on the other side of the china cabinet. You duck around there and put your back to it. You just hope that the ghost boy will think you ran all the way to the kitchen.

You can't help thinking you should have listened to Iris.

A minute passes. Two. The boy hasn't gone past.

You peer around the edge of the china cabinet. There's no sign of him.

A wicked laugh rings out from INSIDE the cabinet!

As you jump back from it, the ghost boy oozes out. "Looking for me?" he giggles.

He moves towards you.

Lurching back, you thump into a chair.

"Did you really think you could hide from a ghost?" he asks.

THE END

You look around desperately for something you can use to defend yourself. The chairs are too heavy. Everything else looks too light.

Then your eyes fall on the small gargoyle that sits in the middle of the fireplace mantle.

Reaching up, you try to pull it down. It tilts forward but then stops. You hear a loud "click" and then a scraping rumble from inside the fireplace!

Looking down, you see the back of the fireplace slide away, revealing a narrow passageway leading off to one side.

Out in the hall, you hear Sue call out softly, "Tim? You okay?"

Then Barry says, "If he's playing some dumb joke, I'm going to kill him."

Suddenly, it seems kind of silly to be looking for a weapon.

As you step into the hall, you hear Sue say, "Why is he so still?"

Then Barry stammers, "Is he . . . is he . . . "

GO ON TO THE NEXT PAGE.

YES, HE IS...

YOU REACH UP TO RUB YOUR EYES. YOU'RE POSITIVE THE BOY WASN'T THERE A SECOND BEFORE.

WHO'S NEXT?

THE BOY GOES INTO TIM'S ROOM. THEN...

AAARRRGGGGHHHH!

HE GOT TIM! HE GOT BARRY!

YOU RUB YOUR EYES AGAIN. THESE PEOPLE JUST... *APPEARED.*

WHAT'S ALL THIS RUCKUS?

WHY ARE YOU RUNNING AWAY?

NOOOOOO!

GO ON TO THE NEXT PAGE.

You duck back into your room, not sure what to do. It's too late to help Sue.

WILL YOU . . .

. . . break the window and try to climb down?
TURN TO PAGE 12.

. . . try to trick the ghosts by breaking the window, then hiding in the passage?
TURN TO PAGE 63.

. . . run straight into the secret passage?
TURN TO PAGE 81.

Maybe you'll find something in the tower to explain what's happening in this house. You go up the stairs. They end at a trap door.

Cautiously, you push the door open. It's heavy, but you manage to raise it.

You lift your candle and peer inside. The room is empty, except for closed book on a wooden lectern in the center.

Curious, you climb up and ease the trap door back into place.

At the lectern, you open the book to a place marked by a velvet ribbon. Reddish dust sprays in your face. Coughing, you wave your hand to clear the air. There is only one sentence on the page: "It was a trap."

You turn to run, but you stumble and fall to the floor, gasping.

TURN TO PAGE 78.

You decide you'd better get a hold of yourself. Hugging the wall, you talk deep breaths. After a few minutes, you feel better.

Carefully, you start to inch along the ledge. Foot by foot, you get nearer to the edge of the house.

Finally, you grasp the corner of the house. You pull yourself around it.

"What took you so long?"

You can't believe it! It's the boy from the hallway.

"H-how?" you gasp. Then you remember—you saw him down on the road! He must be able to leave the house…

He reaches for you. You step back quickly, thinking about the screams of your friends.

Your foot slips off the ledge behind you. For a moment, you teeter there.

Then you topple over the edge, falling into the deep, dark chasm behind Ghost Mansion.

THE END

71

"No one yells like that in their sleep," you say. Reaching out, you grab the doorknob. It feels cold.

You swing the door open and go in. Sue and Barry follow. The room is dark, except for the light coming from the hall.

Tim is huddled on the floor in one corner of the room, his knees drawn up against him and his arms covering his head.

"Tim?" you call out quietly. He doesn't answer.

"What's wrong?" says Sue. "Why is he so . . . still?"

You realize she's right. He's not moving at all.

"Is he . . . is he . . . " stammers Barry.

"Yes," says a small voice behind you.

You all jump, startled. When you spin around, there's a small boy standing in the doorway—he same boy from the road. He has a nasty grin.

"Who's next?" he laughs. Then he comes towards you.

GO ON TO THE NEXT PAGE.

You wonder if the boy knows something about what happened to Tim. He couldn't be the one who hurt Tim, could he?

WILL YOU . . .

. . . try to avoid the boy and get out of there?
TURN TO PAGE 11.

. . . try to question the boy?
TURN TO PAGE 60.

"I'm sorry," you say. "I have to get out of here now. They already got my friends."

Iris nods. "I understand. It was too much to ask."

"How do I get out?" you ask.

She leans towards you, talking softly. "The doctor has done something unnatural to the doors and shutters. They won't open before the sun comes up."

"Then how—"

She smiles. "I don't think the doctor's trick works on plain old glass, though. See, there's one room in the house with plenty of windows and no shutters at all," she says.

She starts towards a nearby door. "Come along," she says. "Quiet as a mouse. We don't want them to hear!"

THAT CHESTER WAS ALWAYS A BAD ONE. BEING A GHOST HASN'T HELPED ANY. FIRST THING HE DID WHEN HE CAME BACK WAS DRIVE HIS POOR MOTHER BATTY!

WHEN THE DOCTOR COULDN'T HELP HER WITH MEDICINE, HE GOT SOME NASTY OLD BOOKS AND TRIED...BLACK MAGIC!

WHEN HE AND THE MRS. DIED, THEY BECAME GHOSTS TOO.

ANYWAY, HERE WE ARE...

NOW YOU BUST OUT THE GLASS AND BE ON YOUR WAY.

WATCH YOURSELF, THOUGH. THERE'S AN AWFUL DROP.

GO ON TO THE NEXT PAGE.

You pick up one of the tables and toss it through the window. The shattering glass sounds tremendously loud.

"Now run, child," says Iris. "Don't you stop until you get well away from here. Remember that Chester can go all the way down to the road!"

You try to thank her, but she just says, "GO!"

She doesn't have to tell you twice. You climb out the window and start running.

As you reach the road, you hear an awful wailing echoing down from the house. You keep running, wishing you had tried to help Iris.

There was at least one good spirit in Ghost Mansion.

THE END

Tim does play dumb jokes sometimes. Do you want
to give him the satisfaction of falling for this one?
Then again, something could really be wrong.

WILL YOU . . .

. . . go inside?
TURN TO PAGE 72.

. . . suggest that you
leave him alone?
TURN TO PAGE 100.

"We have to get to the stairs!" you yell. "Follow me!"

You run right at the boy, who just smiles. Then you jump, diving over his head. You just hope you don't break anything when you land.

As you sail over his head, he reaches up. His hand goes THROUGH your foot.

Your leg goes numb from the knee down. You try to roll when you hit the floor, but your useless leg sends you sprawling.

From the end of the hall, you can hear Sue pounding on the window, unable to get it open.

The boy comes up to you, makes a face and sticks out his tongue.

It's the last thing you see.

THE END

You tiptoe across the game room and around the billiard table. At the door, you stop and listen.

Not hearing anything, you ease open the pocket doors an inch and peer through.

A pale, cold eye stares back at you.

You stagger back, trip, and fall. You just barely keep the candle from falling.

The ghost woman from upstairs steps through the doors. Without opening them.

"Oh, that's so sad," she cries. "Did it hurt?"

Scrambling back, you get some distance from her and leap to your feet.

The ghostly man is standing there!

He laughs and smiles. "Did I surprise you, youngster?" he says. "Were you expecting a ghost to make noise? Silent as the grave, you know."

Then he comes towards you, his face suddenly looking gaunt and his eyes hollow and dark. "Speaking of which," he whispers, "you must be dying to join your friends!"

THE END

YOU GRAB THE CANDLE, HOPING NO ONE WILL NOTICE IT'S GONE.

PULLING ON THE HANDLE SLIDES THE BACK OF THE FIREPLACE INTO PLACE AGAIN. NOW, YOU JUST HOPE THIS PASSAGE WILL LEAD YOU TO A *WAY OUT*!

A DOOR! BUT IS IT SAFE TO USE?

AND A STAIRCASE. WHICH ONE SHOULD YOU TAKE?

TURN TO PAGE 40.

"Let's just see who it is," you say. Reaching up, you tip the gargoyle back. The fireplace closes.

"Wait," says Sue. "Listen."

The four of you stand absolutely still. Moments pass.

Barry whispers, "I don't hear anything."

"That's what I mean," Sue says. "What happened to the noise?"

"I'm going to check the hall," you say softly.

"We should get OUT of here!" mutters Tim.

You, Barry, and Sue all turn toward Tim.

"We get it," Barry says. "You're scared. Now shut up!"

You and Sue nod in agreement.

Tim scowls and starts to argue. Then he looks surprised. His lips move without a sound. He points behind you.

You turn and gasp!

GO ON TO THE NEXT PAGE.

GO ON TO THE NEXT PAGE.

Tim finally manages to speak. "Run!" he yelps.
But do you really need to? Can a ghost even touch
a normal person? He seems excited because
Sue is afraid. Does that mean something?

WILL YOU . . .

. . . try to convince the ghost he doesn't scare you?
TURN TO PAGE 41.

. . . try to escape through the passage?
TURN TO PAGE 97.

. . . try to slip past the ghost and go
through the door?
TURN TO PAGE 110.

You give her a nod. "Let's go."

She leads you back into the secret passage and tells you to close the door. She drifts up the stairs ahead of you, quiet as the grave.

Iris goes past the door at the top of the stairs, to one of the fireplace entrances you passed on your way down. She points at the lever and then oozes through the wall.

You pull the lever and wait for the fireplace to open. Your heart is pounding.

Through the walls, you hear an awful wail of frustration. You freeze.

"Where did the child get to?" a woman's voice calls out. "Come out, come out, wherever you are!"

You can just barely hear a young boy's voice reply, "Quiet, Mother! They get more frightened when you sneak up on them!"

Quickly, you slip out of the passage.

GO ON TO THE NEXT PAGE.

HURRY! HURRY! THE CONTRACTS SHOULD BE IN THE CENTER DRAWER!

QUICKLY! YOU'VE GOT TO FIND THE RIGHT ONES TO BURN!

THERE ARE TOO MANY! THERE'S NOT ENOUGH TIME!

FWOOOSH!

You step back to watch the papers burn, hoping the fire won't spread too fast.

An awful scream echoes through the house! Suddenly, the three Hales appear in the room.

"Too late!" cries Iris. "I'm free!"

"We can still punish your rescuer!" Dr. Hale growls. "You can't stop all of us by yourself!"

The butler appears and grabs hold of the doctor. "She won't have to!" he shouts.

Chester tries to get at you, but Iris has him by the arm. Then she grabs Mrs. Hale too.

"Run!" she yells. "The doctor can't fight Hiller and keep the doors closed too!"

Dodging around the ghosts, you rush into the hallway and down the creaking stairs to the front door.

It opens!

Halfway down the drive, you stop and look back. The flames have spread, engulfing Ghost Mansion and burning it clean.

THE END

Remembering that you saw the ghost boy down on the road, you decide you'd better keep moving.

You inch along the ledge. Closer. Closer.

Finally, you come to the corner of the house and heave yourself around to safer ground.

You want to throw yourself down and hug the ground. Only you keep thinking about that creepy kid. You start to run.

As you reach the road, you hear a small, mean voice howling in frustration behind you.

You run past the car, thinking about your friends.

You keep running in the rain, hoping they won't become more spirits in Ghost Mansion.

THE END

"Sue's right," you say. "Let's go."

Reluctantly, Barry and Tim agree. It doesn't take long to get back to your room.

As you come out of the fireplace, a high-pitched voice exclaims, "You're not supposed to use the passages!"

The boy from the road is in your room!

"Don't be mad," says Sue. "We didn't mean any harm." She walks over to him and hold out her hand. "I'm Sue. What's your name?"

"I'm Chester," says the boy. He puts his small, pale hand into hers.

Sue shivers. Then her arm starts to turn blue!

Chester starts to laugh.

That's when you realize that you can almost see THROUGH him.

You rush over, trying to pull Sue away. Chester just lets go—and puts his hand right into your throat! You try to swallow, to breathe, but you can't.

You fall.

The last thing you see is Chester's smile.

THE END

90

You rush down the stairs as fast as you can in the dark. At the bottom, you shove open the door you find there.

You step out into a kitchen.

Then you realize that someone is standing nearby. With a yelp, you duck away.

A short, plump lady in a plain dress with a white apron over it looks down at you. Her eyes are kind.

"Don't be afraid of old Iris," she says quietly. "I mean you no harm."

You give her a closer look. You can see the door to another room behind her. Through her.

"Y-you're like them," you say. "A ghost."

"A ghost, yes," she says, "but not like them. You have to trust me, child."

Next to you is a door leading farther into the house. Across the kitchen, you see another door that leads outside.

GO ON TO THE NEXT PAGE.

She looks nice, but she's a *ghost*. You can't help thinking about what happened to your friends. Can you trust any ghost?

WILL YOU . . .

. . . ignore her advice and try the outside door?
TURN TO PAGE 14.

. . . take a chance and trust her?
TURN TO PAGE 28.

You make your way carefully down the steps, flinching every time one creaks. With four of you, it happens a lot.

At the bottom of the steps, there's a narrow door.

"Ready?" you ask. The others nod. Slowly, you push the door open, hoping its hinges don't squeal.

You step out into a big, old-fashioned kitchen. Holding a finger to your lips for quiet, you swing the door back into place.

"Well, now, what have we here?"

Tim lets out a yelp, and you all jump back. Someone was standing behind the open door!

A short, plump lady in a plain dress and a white apron looks the four of you up and down. You hold your breath.

She gives you a warm smile.

"Don't be afraid of old Iris," she says quietly. "I mean you no harm. Unlike some I could mention."

She leans forward and whispers, "But we better keep quiet. Otherwise the doctor and the Mrs. might hear."

GO ON TO THE NEXT PAGE.

YOU SHOULD GET OUT OF THIS HOUSE AS QUICKLY AS YOU CAN! IT'S AN *UNWHOLESOME* PLACE.

YOU DON'T HAVE TO TELL ME *TWICE!*

HEY! IT'S LOCKED OR STUCK OR SOMETHING!

THAT'LL BE THE DOCTOR'S DOING. IT WON'T OPEN UNTIL MORNING.

YOU LISTEN CLOSE! STAY AWAY FROM THE HALES. ALL THREE OF THEM.

AND WHATEVER YOU DO, DON'T LET THEM LAY A HAND ON YOU. THEIR TOUCH IS AS *COLD* AS THE *GRAVE.*

GO ON TO THE NEXT PAGE.

"What do you mean?" you ask.

"It started a long time back," she says. "That boy, Chester, was a bad one from the start. Used to go down to the road and jump out in front of automobiles, trying to make people crash their vehicles!"

"Like he did to us!" you say.

She nods. "One day, he dodged one way when he should have gone the other. The driver brought him up to the house, but the doctor couldn't save him."

"B-but, we saw him," says Sue. "He . . . "

"Haven't you guessed?" Iris interrupts. "Everyone here—"

"So there you are!" a voice booms behind you.

Turning, you see the man from the dining room standing in the kitchen doorway. This must be Dr. Hale! He gives a strange smile.

"Chester just went up to see you!" he says. "Come along. You mustn't disappoint him!"

The doctor wants you to go upstairs,
but the cook said to avoid him.

WILL YOU . . .

. . . try to get away?
TURN TO PAGE 22.

. . . do as he asks?
TURN TO PAGE 34.

"The passage!" you shout. You pull the gargoyle forward, activating the hidden door.

The thing seems to move in slow motion. Terrified, you look back. The ghost boy is still standing in the same place, looking puzzled.

You pile into the secret passage with your friends. Behind you, Barry throws the switch to close the fireplace mechanism.

In the darkness, Tim lets out a sigh. "We . . . we got away."

Then a soft glowing light forms ahead of you. The ghostly boy has stepped into the passage. He looks at you, still puzzled.

"I can go through walls, you know. Just like I went through the door to the room."

You try to turn, to go back the way you came. But the passage is narrow and Tim, Sue, and Barry are blocking the way.

You feel icy fingers pushing through your back. "That was too easy," says the ghost boy. "No fun at all."

THE END

GO ON TO THE NEXT PAGE.

"Jump!" yells Barry. He leaps over the banister. You follow him, hoping for a good landing.

Barry hits the floor just a second or two before you do. A cloud of dust swirls up around him, the floor creaks, and you hear a loud *CRACK!* A floorboard gives way, and one of Barry's legs pushes through it.

Your feet slam into the floor.

More floorboards snap beneath you and Barry. The old dry wood can't take the strain of two people dropping down on it so hard!

You slide into the hole in the floor. Ignoring the jab of splinters, you try to grab onto the edge as you fall. You think you might almost . . .

Barry's hand clamps onto your leg. "Hang on!" he yells, desperate and frightened.

His weight is too much.

You both scream as you fall into the damp, cold darkness beneath Ghost Mansion.

THE END

"Maybe he's playing a joke," you say. "Or having a nightmare."

Sue turns back toward her room and says, "I'm going to try to get some sleep."

Barry hangs back for a second. "Maybe I should check."

Behind him, you see something strange happening to Tim's door. Smoke or something is drifting off of the wood. It almost looks like . . .

"A hand!" you yell, pointing behind Barry. He turns around and stares. Behind you, Sue gasps with surprise.

A pale figure steps THROUGH the closed door. It's the boy from the road!

He scowls at the three of you. "You're no fun!" he says.

"This can't be happening," whispers Barry.

The little guy flashes a wicked smile. "Sure it can!"

"This way!" Sue hollers. "There's a window at the end of the hall! We can climb down from there!"

Sue waves for you to come. But can you really
climb down from a second-story window?
Maybe you should just try to slip past
the ghost and head for the stairs.

WILL YOU . . .

. . . make a run for the stairs?
TURN TO PAGE 79.

. . . try to climb out the window?
TURN TO PAGE 90.

Remembering the view from your room, you decide to play it safe. The house stands on a cliff. Crashing through the window could send you over the edge.

Picking up one of the small tables, you hurl it through the window. Glass explodes in a shower of shimmering shards.

Very carefully, you ease out the broken window onto the narrow ledge behind the house. You look down into a deep, dark ravine. It's a very long way down.

Seconds after you begin inching your way along the house, awful moans and shouts echo through the shattered window. Looking back as you ease around the corner, you see Mrs. Hale glaring at you from inside, her fists clenched as she snarls at you.

As you run toward the driveway, you wonder why she isn't coming after you. Maybe she can't leave the place where she died?

GET *BACK* HERE! I'M NOT *DONE* WITH YOU YET!

BUT THE BOY CAN LEAVE THE HOUSE! HE MUST HAVE DIED DOWN AT THE ROAD!

MAYBE *HE* DIED ON THE ROAD, IN THE SPOT WHERE BARRY SWERVED TO MISS HIM!

MAYBE YOU JUST HAVE TO GET PAST THE CAR.

JUST TO BE SAFE, YOU KEEP ON RUNNING.

YOU DON'T WANT TO END UP ANOTHER SPIRIT TRAPPED FOREVER IN GHOST MANSION.

THE END

TURN TO PAGE 77.

You squat down behind one of the chairs in the round room, but you can't bring yourself to blow out the candle. Minutes tick by slowly.

You can't help thinking about your friends. What will you tell their parents? Will you even see your own parents again?

Finally, you can't stand the waiting. You get up and . . .

The ghost man from upstairs is sitting in one of the chairs across the room!

"Hello there," he says. "I'm Dr. Hale. I was wondering just how long you could stay back there. You didn't do badly for a youngster."

"W-why are you doing this?" you stammer. "What did we ever do to you?"

He drifts up out of the chair, coming closer.

"Nothing at all," he replies. "It's what we do. Bad ghosts, I mean."

His drifts closer, reaching for you. "This is the closest thing we have to fun."

THE END

There doesn't seem to be a handle on the door, so you push on it gently. It pivots open, creaking and scraping. You can feel your friends cringe, wondering if someone heard.

Beyond the door is a circular room. A stone staircase to your right leads down, and another to your left leads up. The walls of the room are covered by bookcases crammed with books of all sizes. Several more are open on a large wooden table in the middle of the room. The whole place smells musty, dusty, and unused.

Tim pushes past you. He looks back with a sheepish grin. "I don't like tight places, okay?"

"What is this place?" asks Sue. She wanders over to the table and peers at the books there. She looks puzzled. "I can't read any of this."

You look over her shoulder at the strange characters filling the pages.

"Me neither," you say.

IT DOESN'T LOOK LIKE ANYONE HAS BEEN HERE IN A WHILE. MAYBE WE CAN JUST HIDE OUT HERE UNTIL MORNING?

I DON'T KNOW. I MEAN, IF THEY REALIZE WE'RE GONE, WON'T THEY CHECK THE WHOLE PLACE?

THIS IS *STUPID!* THESE PEOPLE LET US IN AND GAVE US A PLACE TO STAY THE NIGHT. NOW WE'RE POKING AROUND THEIR HOUSE LIKE... LIKE THIEVES OR SOMETHING.

WE SHOULD GO BACK DOWN THAT PASSAGE *RIGHT NOW!*

GO ON TO THE NEXT PAGE.

You wonder if Sue could be right. Maybe the stormy night and the spooky house are making you all nervous for no reason. Then again, the people here do seem kind of strange.

WILL YOU . . .

. . . stay in the tower library?
TURN TO PAGE 39.

. . . go back through the secret passage and to your room?
TURN TO PAGE 89.

You decide that you're better off in the secret passage. If the ghosts don't know that you know about it, they might not look for you there.

Stepping into the passage, you pull the door closed behind you. As you turn to the stairs, your candle reflects off something white. Suddenly, the woman from the hallway lurches out of the shadows right at you!

You jerk back, out of her reach. Your foot hits empty air. The stairs!

As you fall backward, you hear her laughing. "Oh, no!" she cries. "Poor little thing."

You hear her begin to wail as you tumble down the stairs. The candle flies from your hand and goes out. You finish your fall in darkness.

At the bottom, your head smacks into the floor.

Then you don't feel anything at all.

THE END

The ghostly boy drifts forward, his hands stretched out to grab you. Just barely, you manage to dodge his pale, grasping fingers.

"Come on!" you yell back to your friends.

You throw open the door to the hallway. Terrified, Tim pushes past you and runs for the stairs.

By the time you reach them, he's halfway to the bottom. Behind you, Sue screams!

You turn to go back. Then you hear Tim yelp with fear. Looking downstairs, you see a tall, pale man in an old-style suit clutching at Tim.

There's another scream in the hallway. The ghost boy is standing over Barry, smiling.

You turn back toward Tim. The man is right next to you!

"Boo!" he says, smiling.

You stumble. Your foot slips on the top stair and you tumble down.

At the bottom, your head hits the floor with a loud crack.

THE END

YOU ASK HER WHAT YOU CAN DO.

THANK YOU, CHILD. I HOPE THIS WORKS OUT FOR US BOTH. AND HILLER TOO.

SEE, HE HAD HILLER AND ME SIGN CONTRACTS WHEN WE HIRED ON WITH HIM. SAID WE'D SERVE HIM AS LONG AS HE RESIDED IN THIS HOUSE. IT SEEMED LIKE A PROMISE OF LIFETIME EMPLOY.

BUT WHEN HE DIED, HE CAME BACK AS A GHOST. WE COULDN'T LEAVE-- EVEN WHEN *WE DIED.*

BUT IF YOU COULD GET THOSE CONTRACTS FROM HIS DESK UPSTAIRS IN HIS STUDY AND BURN 'EM!? THEN WE'D BE *FREE.* AND WE'D GIVE HIM WHAT FOR, I'LL TELL YOU!

TURN TO PAGE 53.

READY FOR MORE ADVENTURES?

WHICH **TWISTED JOURNEYS™** WILL YOU TRY NEXT?

#1 CAPTURED BY PIRATES
Danger on the high seas! A band of scurvy pirates has boarded your ship. Can you keep them from turning you into shark bait?

#2 ESCAPE FROM PYRAMID X
You're on an archaeological mission to an ancient pyramid, complete with ancient mummies. Unfortunately for you, not everything that's ancient is also dead...

#3 TERROR IN GHOST MANSION
Halloween's not supposed to be *this* scary. You and your friends are trapped in a creepy old house with a bunch of spooks. And they definitely aren't wearing costumes...

#4 THE TREASURE OF MOUNT FATE
Plenty of people have braved the monsters and magic of Mount Fate in search of its legendary treasure. But no one has ever lived to brag about their quest. Will you be the first?